MARCUS PFISTER was born in Bern, Switzerland. After studying at the Art School of Bern, he apprenticed as a graphic designer and worked in an advertising agency before becoming self-employed in 1984. His debut picture book, *The Sleepy Owl*, was published by NorthSouth in 1986, but his big breakthrough came six years later with *The Rainbow Fish*. To date, Marcus has illustrated over sixty-five books, which have been translated into more than sixty languages and received countless international awards. He lives with his wife, Debora, and their children in Bern.

First published in the United States, Great Britain, Canada, Australia, and New Zealand in 2022
by NorthSouth Books Inc., an imprint of NordSüd Verlag AG, CH-8050 Zürich, Switzerland.
Distributed in the United States by NorthSouth Books Inc., New York 10016.
Library of Congress Cataloging-in-Publication Data is available.

ISBN: 978-0-7358-4500-8
1 3 5 7 9 · 10 8 6 4 2

Printed in China
www.northsouth.com

www.rainbowfish.us

Meet Marcus Pfister at www.marcuspfister.ch

Marcus Pfister

RAINBOW FISH
and the Storyteller

Translated by
David Henry Wilson

North
South

Rainbow Fish had been enjoying a little snooze when he was startled out of his dreams by a big fish with an impressive dorsal fin.

"Are you Rainbow Fish?" the new fish asked.

"That's just who I am," said Rainbow Fish. "Who are you?"

"My name is Humbert, and I've got something important to tell you."

"What is this important something you want to tell me?" said Rainbow Fish.

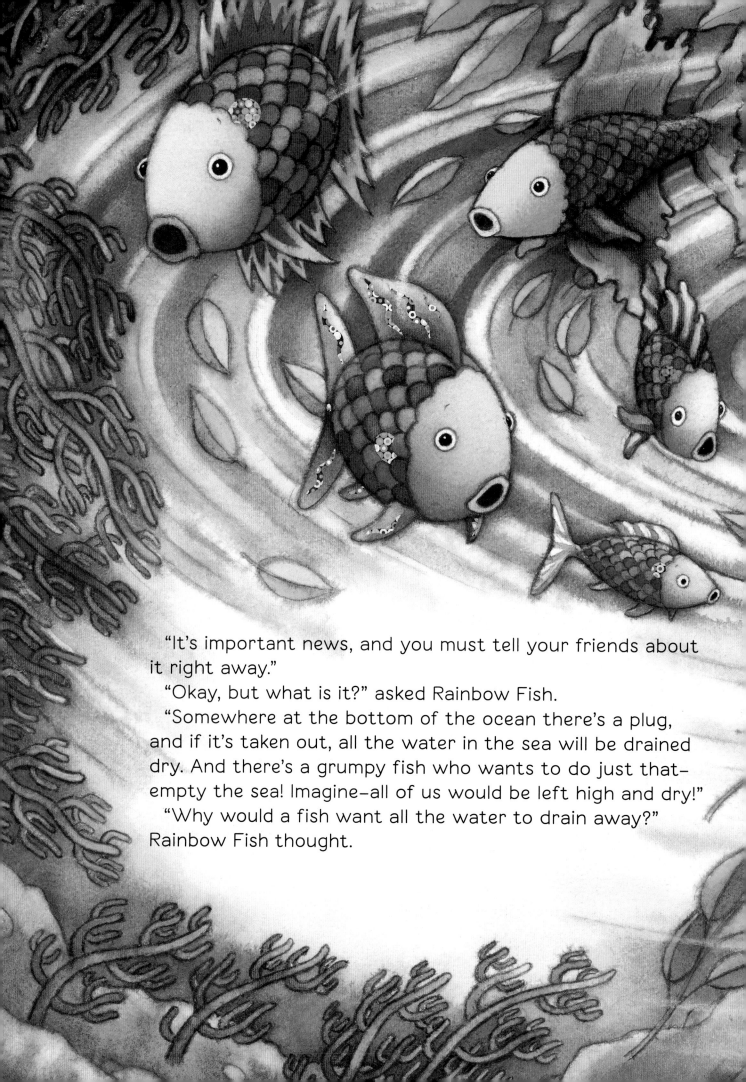

"It's important news, and you must tell your friends about it right away."

"Okay, but what is it?" asked Rainbow Fish.

"Somewhere at the bottom of the ocean there's a plug, and if it's taken out, all the water in the sea will be drained dry. And there's a grumpy fish who wants to do just that—empty the sea! Imagine—all of us would be left high and dry!"

"Why would a fish want all the water to drain away?" Rainbow Fish thought.

"It's much worse than you can imagine," said Humbert. "But I've also got some good news."

"What's that?" asked Rainbow Fish.

"I can help you! I'll protect you! I won't allow anyone to do such a terrible thing! So swim to your friends and tell them all. There's no time to lose!"

Rainbow Fish couldn't make up his mind what to do.
The whole story sounded strange and a bit unbelievable.
All the same, he swam to his friends and told them about his meeting with Humbert.

"I never knew there was a plug," said one fish.

"A plug?!" said another with a laugh. "He must be kidding."

"There isn't really such a plug, is there?" asked the little blue fish.

"That's ridiculous!" said Red Fin. "He must be teasing you to think up a story like that! Tomorrow let's all go and see him together."

The next morning, Rainbow Fish called, "He's coming!" And indeed Humbert was swimming straight toward them.

"Good morning, dear fish," Humbert called out cheerfully. "How are you all?"

"Hello, Humbert," said Rainbow Fish. "I told my friends what you're upset about, but perhaps you can tell them the story of the plug yourself."

"Plug? What sort of plug? What are you talking about? There's something much more important now. On the other side of the rocks there are several shoals of fish that are threatening us. We must stop them from taking over our territory!" said Humbert.

Rainbow Fish and his friends looked at one another in astonishment. Threatening? Taking over? What was this fish talking about?

"What should we do?" asked the little blue fish.

"Don't worry, I've come up with a plan. I'll protect you all!" answered Humbert.

"And how are you going to do that?" asked the fish with the jagged fins.

"Very simple," said Humbert. "We'll use algae and coral to keep them out."

"This sounds like a fairy-tale fantasy," said Red Fin.

"How do we know if he's telling the truth?" asked the yellow fish.

"Suppose it is the truth?" asked another.

"The story about the plug was made up," said Rainbow Fish. "Why should we believe him this time?"

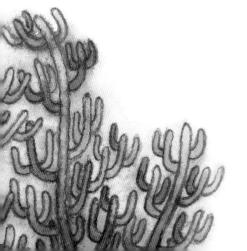

The very next day, Humbert had more alarming news to share. "There's a blue whale living near here. He eats plankton like we do, and he's going to eat up all our food!"

Rainbow Fish laughed. "We've heard that story before. The whale is a good friend of ours, and there's enough food for all of us."

From then on, Rainbow Fish and his friends were very careful not to believe what Humbert told them.

As soon as he started telling an exaggerated story, the friends would laugh. The fish with the jagged fins said, "Humbug, Humbert!"

"Leave him alone," said Red Fin. "He's acting like a silly storyteller. You don't have to take any of his tales seriously."

One day, Red Fin and Rainbow Fish saw Humbert all alone by the rocks.

"Somehow I feel sorry for him," said Red Fin. "He's always on his own now. Can't we do something to help him?"

"Maybe he could use his storytelling talent in a different way," said Rainbow Fish. "We all like listening to fairy tales and adventures, but he shouldn't pretend that his stories are true."

The two of them swam to Humbert and told him about their idea. He was very enthusiastic.

"Storyteller? Why not? I have so many ideas!"

"But you understand, we don't want to hear any more lies or tall tales to scare us, right?" said Rainbow Fish.

"Yes, okay," mumbled Humbert. "I think I'll be able to make up nice stories too."

"That's great!" said Red Fin. "Let's start storytelling time today!"

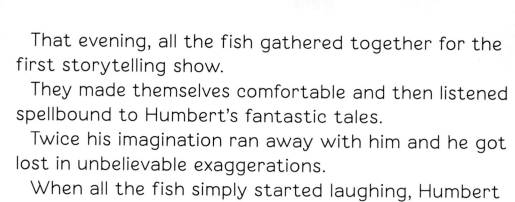

That evening, all the fish gathered together for the first storytelling show.

They made themselves comfortable and then listened spellbound to Humbert's fantastic tales.

Twice his imagination ran away with him and he got lost in unbelievable exaggerations.

When all the fish simply started laughing, Humbert went red in the face and quickly found his way back into the story.

It was not long before none of the fish ever wanted to miss a single storytelling time with Humbert.